KLONDIKE ARTHUR

THE ARTHUR BOOKS

Railroad Arthur
Arthur the Kid
Buffalo Arthur
The Lone Arthur
Klondike Arthur

★ ALAN COREN ★

KLONDIKE ARTHUR

Illustrated by John Astrop

Little, Brown and Company
Boston   Toronto

FIRST AMERICAN EDITION

T 04/78

Library of Congress Cataloging in Publication Data

Coren, Alan, 1938–
    Klondike Arthur.

    SUMMARY: It takes a ten-year-old bard to reform
Grizzly Wilkinson, the meanest prospector in the
Klondike gold fields.
    [1.   Klondike gold fields—Fiction.
2.   Gold mines and mining—Fiction.   3.   Friendship
—Fiction]   I.   Astrop, John.   II.   Title.
PZ7.C81538Kl   1979   [Fic]   78–23176
ISBN 0–316–15733–3

PRINTED IN THE UNITED STATES OF AMERICA

For Stefanie

★

ONCE upon a time, a little over a hundred years ago, in the far Northwest of North America (so far north, in fact, that it was as close to the North Pole as it was to the United States!), a very odd deal took place.

The Russians sold Alaska to the Americans!

If it seems somewhat strange to us today that a piece of territory more than ten times the size of England should be bought and sold, remember that it wasn't quite so strange in 1867 when this particular sale was made. Powerful countries then tended to do pretty much as they liked with things they considered belonged to them by right.

It wouldn't be so easy to make such a sale today.

Especially at the price. Because Alaska was

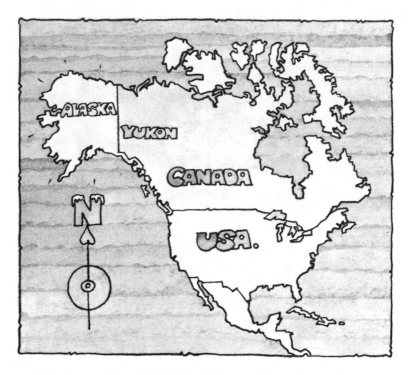

sold for only $7,200,000; and although over seven million dollars sounds like an enormous amount of money, it actually worked out at exactly two cents per acre, which is a very *tiny* amount of money. To give you some idea, at that price you could buy Disneyland for a dollar and a half!

Why on earth did the Russians let Alaska go so cheaply, is what you're probably wondering.

2

That was exactly the question the Russians were asking themselves just a few years later, at about the time this story begins. The Russians had believed they were selling half a million square miles of ice and bare rocks and

tundra and reindeer; a wasteland, in short, and a bleak and freezing and uninhabitable one, at that. What they didn't know was that in 1880 a lonely fur trapper trying to eke out a living along the icy banks of the Yukon River would one day dig out a hole to build himself a shelter against the piercing wind.

And that he would notice, when he'd finished, something at the bottom of that hole.

Something which had once been a hidden part of the brown-black rock that surrounded it, but which time and the constant movement of underground water had gradually separated,

3

until it lay exposed, like a dull yellow walnut. Not much to look at, but in the years that followed its discovery, many thousands of men would flock to the Yukon, ready to die and, worse, ready to kill, just to get their greedy hands on it.

For it was gold!

Because it was gold, that one nugget meant that the Alaskan earth might be full of it. So no sooner had the news broken than all over America men left their jobs, their wives, their children, and in many cases left their senses, too. They grabbed shovels and picks and, unfortunately, guns, and began to scurry north just as fast as their mules and wagons and legs could carry them. The Great Alaskan Gold Rush had started! And for every man who hoped to make an honest strike and find his own gold, there was another who had no intention of doing any prospecting at all, but planned instead to steal the gold that others dug.

Men were killed — and not only for their gold. So lawless, so wicked, so very, very crazy were the Gold Rush towns, that men shot one another for their boots, for their earmuffs, or simply for not saying "Good morning." In the saloons, waiters were shot for putting their thumbs in the soup, and barmen were shot for forgetting who ordered whiskey and who ordered beer. In the barbershops, barbers were shot for cutting off too much hair, or too little. And as for dentists who pulled out the wrong tooth . . .

In short, just about the best way to get rich

quickly in Alaska was to forget about digging for gold altogether and open an undertaker's business!

And just about the *second* best way to get rich quickly was to run a saloon. For after a hard day's prospecting, the one thing every miner wanted to do was come in from the terrible skin-cracking cold, into a place with a roaring stove and cheerful company. They all wanted someplace to buy a drink to warm the blood and bring the circulation back to frozen fingers and red noses and blue ears, someplace with a piano, where men sang songs and told jokes and swapped stories of the day's doings amid the bleak blackness of the mines and the bleak whiteness of the snow.

The piano was very important indeed. No saloon could stay in business long without a piano, and if you think about it for a moment, I'm sure you'll understand why. Can you imagine what life would be like without music? Without songs to cheer you up when you were sad, and songs to celebrate with when you were happy? If you can imagine how grim it was to be a miner in terrible lost Alaska, a thousand miles from anywhere, and even farther from the friends and families you'd left behind, well, it's not difficult to see how much the gold miners needed music to brighten things up. Especially since miners were roughly divided into two sorts: those who'd found gold, and those who hadn't. In other words, those who were extremely cheerful and wanted to sing, and those who were extremely miserable and wanted cheering up.

Which was why the pianist of the Rotten Old Saloon in Dogsnose Gap was such a very important man.

There was a reason, of course, why the Rotten Old Saloon was called that and why the town was called Dogsnose Gap.

The truth of the matter was that the Gold Rush towns sprang up very quickly. One moment there would be nothing but a flat stretch of snow, the next it would be filled by wooden huts and loony miners rushing about digging and shooting and drinking and singing, and so on. Now, the first man to arrive in Dogsnose Gap, before, of course, it was called anything at all, was a man by the name of R. B. Flink. He was accompanied by his friend James Rumbold, and since they had come from California, which is a warm and soft and sunny state, the first thing that struck them was the fearful weather.

"This place," announced R. B. Flink, dismounting from his mule and slapping his frostbitten hands together, "is colder than a dog's nose!"

They stared together at the unending whiteness.

8

"I wonder what it's called," said James Rumbold.

"It's not called anything," replied R. B. Flink.

"It'll have to be called something soon," said James Rumbold.

"Then," said R. B. Flink, "we'll call it — hang on — Dogsnose Gap!"

And that was that.

Later more miners arrived. Then builders and carpenters and gamblers and barmen and cooks and barbers and undertakers and all the rest poured in, so that in less time than it takes to tell, Dogsnose Gap was a thriving shanty town.

And of all the ramshackle buildings, with their rough-planked walls and their tarred-felt roofs and their lopsided windows and their crooked tin chimneys, the most important — apart, of course, from the undertaker's — was the Rotten Old Saloon.

Naturally, it had not been named the Rotten Old Saloon by the man who owned it. He was a rather fat, rather plum-faced, rather pompous man from San Francisco, who knew that prospectors would pay almost anything to get a drink. So when the Alaskan Gold Rush started, he had sped north in the hope of making his own pile of gold without actually having to dig for it, and opened a place called Hubert Tiddle's Amazing Pleasure Palace.

Named, of course, after himself, since Hubert Tiddle was as vain as he was pompous.

He painted the wooden front of his saloon in green and gold and crimson; he draped it with flags, and he announced a Grand Gala Opening, all to attract customers.

But he didn't spend much money on the inside, and when he threw open the doors on Gala Day and the great mob of prospectors burst through, they stopped in their tracks. Far from being a pleasure palace, it was just a long bar and a scattering of bare wooden tables, with sawdust on the floor instead of a carpet.

"Why," cried the miners, "it's just a rotten old saloon!"

10

And, much to Hubert Tiddle's annoyance, the name stuck.

Still, it *was* the only saloon in Dogsnose Gap, and when it was full of customers, it was a pretty cheery spot, with a great log fire crackling away at one end and at the other, most important, a piano. All day long, and all night, too, the old piano rocked and jangled, pouring out glad songs and sad songs, comic songs and serious songs, filling not just the saloon but also the heads and hearts of all who came to drink there with tunes and cheer. The pianist was none other than Memory Nobbs, called that because he had not only heard more tunes than anyone else in America, that is to say one thousand two hundred and thirty-four, *he could also remember one thousand two hundred and thirty-three of them!*

Memory Nobbs was small and very thin, with long delicate fingers that had been flattened at their tips, like teaspoons, from all the long years of playing, and his face was mostly smile, because he liked nothing better than making other people feel good. And up there along the Klondike, Memory Nobbs made people feel very good indeed.

In fact, he had only one other expression besides his enormous smile, and that was a sort of

mild puzzlement, a pursing of the lips, a furrowing of the brow, a very slight shake of the head. He had this expression for only about a minute or so a day, but he did have it *every* day, and that was because, as you may have guessed, it was the expression which came on when he was trying to remember the one thousand two hundred and thirty-fourth tune.

Did it go something like this? Or perhaps something like that? Did it start high up, PING? Or low down, BONG?

It was no use: try as he might, whistle though he did, hum, run up and down the scale, and lie awake sometimes sorting out notes in his head, Memory Nobbs just couldn't quite remember it.

Then he would shake his head, and laugh, and tell himself that it really didn't matter, and he'd start thumping away at one of the other one thousand two hundred and thirty-three. The miners would sing and stamp their feet and forget the cold, the disappointment, and the fact that their loved ones were a thousand

miles away. The Rotten Old Saloon would rock
and rattle and tinkle to Memory Nobbs and his
miraculous piano.

Until, that is, that terrible night in No-
vember.

It had been one of Dogsnose Gap's better
days.

Eleven prospectors had made gold strikes,
which was more than usual. This always
cheered everyone up, even the most envious
ones, because it meant there was still plenty of
gold around and if you just kept on searching
and digging and panning and praying, then one
day . . .

So the Rotten Old Saloon was even noisier
than usual, with eleven prospectors celebrating
and buying drinks for everyone else, including
Memory Nobbs, who was therefore kept so
busy in playing request numbers as a way of
saying thank you that he had to play everything twice as fast as normal, just to get them
all in.

14

He was halfway through "Dixie," which was everybody's favorite Civil War song. The prospectors were marching up and down the long sawdusty floor in ranks of three — their shovels over their shoulders and their voices making all the glasses on the bar jiggle up and down — when the door to the street flew open and the fearful Klondike gale howled through the room on a whirling shower of snow.

The miners spun around, ready to shoot whoever had been inconsiderate enough to leave the door open; but when they saw who it was, they stopped stock-still, as if the whistling wind had suddenly frozen them where they stood.

Their singing died in their throats!

Their eyes goggled in their heads!

The only movement in the room was that of Memory Nobbs's fingers as they flew up and down the keyboard, and the only sound above the wind was that of Memory Nobbs's tinkling notes.

For Memory Nobbs had been too absorbed in his playing to notice that the enormous thing

framed in the doorway was none other than
Grizzly Wilkinson!

Grizzly Wilkinson was so terrible that he
was generally considered to be not only the
most terrible man in Alaska but also the second
and third most terrible, too.

If anyone began to list the terrible things

that Grizzly Wilkinson had done, you would in all probability faint dead away; so just for the record, know that he had earned his strange name on one typically terrible day when a giant grizzly bear had wandered into his camp and attempted to steal his breakfast. Whereupon Algernon Wilkinson (as he was then known) walked up to the grizzly bear, knocked it flat with a single blow of his enormous fist, then sat down on it to finish his breakfast.

So you can see why no one dared tell him to shut the door. They just stood there, shivering — and not just with the cold, either.

Grizzly Wilkinson strode into the room, looking — since his giant body was covered in a black bearskin coat and his giant face was all but covered in black beard and hair — like a grizzly himself. His staring yellow eyes, blazing out of the black hairy mass, never left Memory Nobbs, still pounding his piano and bouncing up and down cheerily on his piano stool.

The terrible mouth of Grizzly Wilkinson opened: "I DON'T LIKE MUSIC!" he roared.

"I wish I was in Dixie, hooray, hooray!" sang

Memory Nobbs, still not looking up. "In Dixie-land I'll take my stand, to live and . . ."

The reason he stopped was that he suddenly found himself several feet above the ground, with his little legs dangling and his face pressed up against the terrible beard of Grizzly Wilkinson. Memory Nobbs's famous smile sort of, well, fell off. The mouth that it had just left opened and shut, but nothing came out. With one enormous hand, Grizzly Wilkinson held him clear of the ground, and with the other he tapped Memory Nobbs on the chest.

"When I say I don't like music," growled Grizzly Wilkinson, and though his growl was quieter than his roar it was somehow even more terrible, "what I *mean* is **I don't like music!**"

Whereupon he walked slowly across to a row of pegs, hung Memory Nobbs on one of them beside the miners' coats, walked back to the piano, lifted it above his black head without even grunting, and tossed it into a corner with no more effort than if it had been a sack of feathers.

18

The beautiful piano landed with one of the most heartbreaking noises it is possible to hear, a jangling mixture of BOINGS and DONGS, BANGS and TWANGS as everything inside it exploded into a thousand pieces and collapsed into a splintery heap of firewood with a last pitiful PING!

Before the horror-stricken miners had recov-

19

ered from the shock (not that they would have dared to do anything about it), Grizzly Wilkinson had stomped back through the room and out again into the freezing blackness. He slammed the door with such force that the unfortunate Memory Nobbs was jolted from his peg and deposited upon the floor beneath.

He buried his face in his delicate hands. "Why did he do it?" he cried.

"Because," said a miner darkly, "he is Grizzly Wilkinson."

The others nodded.

No other explanation was needed.

"There isn't another piano for a hundred miles!" cried Memory Nobbs. "And *that* one belongs to No-Nose Muldoon, who wears two guns and shoots anyone who asks him to play 'Down by the Old Mill Stream.' Not the sort of man you could get a piano away from at all! It'll take six months to get another one."

The miners stared at the floor, not daring to think what life would be like without music.

Gloom descended on the Rotten Old Saloon, a thick miserable silence punctuated only by grunts and sighs and low sad mumbles as the miners grew sorrier and sorrier for themselves. Even sorrier than all his customers was Hubert Tiddle, who had enough experience about gold-rush saloons to know that unless prospectors were given some sort of entertainment to take their minds off their troubles, pretty soon they'd start making their own entertainment, which simply meant that they'd start chucking tables through his windows and shooting holes in his mirrors.

Which was almost exactly what happened, with the slight but important difference that it was through Hubert Tiddle himself that his customers decided to shoot holes!

Unable to get back at anyone for wrecking their piano, since they were all so terrified of Grizzly Wilkinson, they decided to put the blame on poor Hubert Tiddle. They stood him on the table, while he wriggled and shrieked, and they nailed his boots to the tabletop so he couldn't move. They took out their revolvers, they threw a coin to see who would get first shot, they stood in a line waiting their turn be-

hind the winner, and they aimed their guns, and . . .

And who knows what awful things might

have happened if, at that very moment, a small, yet very clear and very strong, voice had not announced, from somewhere behind them: "I SHOULD LIKE TO RECITE AN ENGLISH-TYPE POEM ENTITLED *I'D MUCH RATHER HAVE MY MUMMY THAN ALL THE GOLD IN THE WORLD* BY ARTHUR WILLIAM FOSKETT!"

The miners paused!

The miners stared at one another!

Had their ears deceived them?

Had someone said he was going to recite a poem?

They turned, guns still out. There, on the stairs that led up to the bedrooms, stood a small boy of about ten. The miners gasped! Even Hubert Tiddle, who had put his hands over his face in terror, opened his fingers to peep through at the interruption.

The small boy looked at them all very calmly, and cleared his throat. He did not seem in the least bit scared of these dreadful men, who normally shot people who interrupted them. Before the miners could recover from their shock enough to complain that what they wanted was a piano and not a recitation, the small boy began!

"Last night, by the Klondike River,
I dug up a fortune in gold!
But I caught a chill on my liver,
Brought on by the bitter cold!

24

It was far too late to push on,
So I placed the sack at my head;
But gold makes a very hard cushion,
And ice makes a very cold bed.

So I stared at the stars above me,
As my freezing body lay;
And thought of the folk who loved me,
A thousand miles away.

The voice of my dear old mother
Seemed to cry from the icy rocks:
'I told you to wear another
Sweater, and extra socks!'

My body is stiff. I shall die here,
In this lonely Klondike ditch;
And all I can think as I lie here,
Is: why did I want to be rich?

There's a block of ice in my tummy,
And my frozen toes have curled.
Oh, I'd much rather have my mummy
Than all the gold in the world!"

When the small boy finished, he bowed.
There was a very long silence. Then, as one
by one the miners took out their red polka dot

handkerchiefs, there came the sound of sad noses being blown, and deep sighs being sighed, and, here and there, a sob or two being sobbed. Slowly, the miners replaced their guns in their holsters; slowly, they detached Hubert Tiddle, who was also crying softly, and lowered him gently to the ground.

Then Ironface Sam McGhee, the toughest miner of all, who had six different knife scars on each cheek and a deep dent in his forehead from a shovel fight, looked up at the small boy, and said: "That was the most beautiful poem I have ever heard!"

And everyone agreed, nodding as they snuffled, murmuring as they wept.

"Who is this Arthur William Foskett?" asked Ironface Sam McGhee.

"I am," said the small boy.

"*WHAT?*" cried the miners.

Hubert Tiddle, recovering remarkably quickly from his fearful ordeal, rushed up and grasped Arthur's hands in his.

"Did I hear right?" he yelled. "Do you know more poems, too?"

"Oh, yes," replied Arthur. "As a matter of fact, I have written one hundred and forty-seven. They're probably not very good," he added quickly, in case anyone should think he was boasting. "I just thought it looked like the sort of moment when a poem might take people's minds off doing something pretty awful. I mean, I wouldn't normally dream of pushing myself forward like that and making people listen to me."

"Nonsense!" exclaimed Hubert Tiddle, who was recovering more rapidly every second, now that he had spotted what looked like another golden opportunity to make money. "Why, you could make this the most famous saloon in all Alaska! There's nothing miners like more than a little light entertainment, and now we haven't got a piano anymore, good heavens! — you could make all the difference to my, er, I mean, to *their* lives."

Arthur looked at him.

"What about Mr. Nobbs?" he inquired.

"Oh, *him!*" said Hubert Tiddle, waving his

hand airily. "Don't worry about him. What good's a pianist without a piano?"

"That," said Arthur firmly, "is most unfair. It isn't his fault his piano got smashed. You'll have to continue paying him if you want me to do recitations. You don't," continued Arthur, as he saw Hubert Tiddle's plump face go suddenly white, "have to pay *me*. I'll do it for the fun of it."

At this, Hubert Tiddle brightened again, even though he could not possibly understand why anyone would want to do anything for nothing; but, then, that was only one of the many differences between Arthur and Hubert Tiddle. So Hubert Tiddle said, very quickly, in case Arthur should change his mind: "Done!"

They shook hands on the deal, and Hubert Tiddle, not at all surprisingly, beamed from one fat pink ear to the other.

"Tell you what," he said, his little eyes glowing, "we'll put up a big sign outside the saloon! THE GREAT FOSKETT: POEMS RECITED WHILE YOU WAIT!"

Arthur shook his head.

"I shouldn't like to be called the Great any-thing," he said. "Everybody would think I was showing off, and they'd be right. What about THE ORDINARY FOSKETT?"

"Don't be silly!" snapped Hubert Tiddle. "Who'd want to listen to anybody ordinary?"

It was at this point that Memory Nobbs strolled up, dusting the sawdust from his green velvet vest. His famous smile was back, and he shook Arthur's hand warmly.

"Couldn't help overhearing," he said, "and though I don't like to brag, I probably know as much about show business as anyone around, and my personal opinion, based on a lifetime of experience, is that you ought to call yourself Klondike Arthur. It's got a very nice ring to it."

Arthur turned the words over in his head, thoughtfully.

"You're absolutely right, Mr. Nobbs," he said. "I shall take the stage name of Klondike Arthur. But," he added sternly, looking straight into Hubert Tiddle's eyes, "not in very large letters. And you'll have to put ASSISTED BY MR. MEMORY NOBBS."

"Oh my!" cried Memory Nobbs. "That's remarkably kind of you."

"Well," replied Arthur, "I'm only helping out until you get a new piano, after all."

"Wonderful," said Memory Nobbs. "I shall make it my job to announce you, keep the audience quiet, turn over your pages, and so forth."

"Thank you," said Arthur, "but it won't be necessary to turn pages. I know all the poems by heart."

"What!" exclaimed Memory Nobbs. "It's a good thing I got my name first, else we'd have to call you Memory Foskett. My word, I've just thought of something. You don't happen to remember a tune that sort of goes a bit like, er . . ."

"GIVE US A POEM!" roared a voice in the mob at the bar.

For the miners, who had cheered themselves up after Arthur's sad poem with a number of large drinks, were ready for another. A hundred bearded faces turned toward Arthur; it was like looking, he thought, at an army of porcupines.

"Better make it a cheerful one," hissed Hubert Tiddle. He mopped his face, suddenly remembering his narrow escape. "You know what they're like if they get too gloomy."

"Right!" barked Memory Nobbs, very professionally. He jumped on a table, and whistled sharply between his teeth, and held up his hands.

"Ladies and gentlemen," he began, "I . . ."

"WHAT?" roared the miners.

"I mean, gentlemen and gentlemen," said Memory Nobbs, "I take pleasure, in company with Mr. Hubert Tiddle, proprietor of this splendid establishment, in presenting for your entertainment and instruction, the greatest poet in the" — he caught Arthur's stern eye — "the greatest poet in Dogsnose Gap:

the one, the only, the amazing — KLONDIKE ARTHUR!"

He stepped down in a thunder of cheering and stamping and clapping, and Arthur took his place on the table.

"In a lighter vein," he said, since it was a phrase he had always rather liked, though he wasn't sure why, "I should like to recite a short poem entitled 'A Klondike Disaster.'"

"What?" muttered Hubert Tiddle, who was standing by Arthur's feet. "I thought you said it was going to be funny."

"It is," replied Arthur, "or, at any rate, it's supposed to be!"

"GET ON WITH IT!" roared the miners.

Arthur squared his shoulders, and began:

"*A miner named Archibald Jolly*
Struck it rich, and went right off his trolley!
  He was so mad for gold,
  He neglected the cold,
And now he's the world's biggest lolly!"

It is said that as Arthur finished his poem, the

shriek of laughter that came out of the hundred assembled throats echoed so far across the Alaskan night that miners at the bottom of their holes five miles away suddenly looked up,

wondering if an avalanche was starting! It is said that packs of Arctic wolves, hearing the strange noise rolling toward them, began to howl themselves, throwing back their heads, and that the howls rose and fell from pack to pack, like a siren, until the laugh that began in the Rotten Old Saloon had set all Alaska going, and the very polar bears, right up beyond the Arctic Circle at the North Pole itself, reared up on their hind legs in surprise and didn't sit down again for an hour!

The miners screamed! The miners choked! The miners fell on the floor, clutching their sides and rolling about until the sawdust inside was whirling as much as the snowflakes out-side! And no sooner had the laughter begun to die down into helpless gasping, than one miner would catch another's eye and cry "WORLD'S BIGGEST LOLLY!" and the whole thing would start up all over again!

Klondike Arthur looked at them.

"It wasn't *that* funny," he murmured.

Memory Nobbs wiped the tears from his eyes.

"Oh yes it was!" he gasped. "Don't forget, we've all been out here for ages. We haven't heard any new jokes for a year!"

Slowly, the miners struggled to their feet,

called for more beer, and slapped one another on the back. They came up to Arthur, beaming and chuckling and shaking his hand.

And as for Hubert Tiddle, his entire head was glowing like a great pink lantern!

"Amazing!" he cried. "Amazing!"

"Thank you very much," said Arthur. "May I go now?"

"Go?" exclaimed Hubert Tiddle. "The evening's just beginning! You said you knew a hundred and forty-seven poems."

"I do," replied Arthur, "but it's my bedtime. I go to bed at half-past eight sharp, except for Saturdays, when I stay up till nine o'clock."

"Well, *we'll* allow you to stay up as late as you like!" cried Hubert Tiddle. "This is Alaska, and anything goes!"

"I know," said Arthur, "and that's one of the things that's wrong with it. It isn't a question of allowing, Mr. Tiddle. I go to bed at eight-thirty because I want a good night's sleep."

"Oh, please!" wheedled Hubert Tiddle. "Just one more poem, just a little one, please stay up for just five more minutes!"

How odd, thought Arthur, to have a grown-up begging a young boy to stay up for five more minutes, instead of the other way around! It was certainly true, as everyone said, that Alaska did strange things to people. He sighed.

"All right, Mr. Tiddle, but *only* five minutes. I don't want to have you saying afterwards 'Oh just another five minutes' and all that kind of nonsense."

Hubert Tiddle nodded, and Memory Nobbs jumped up on the table again. Immediately, the miners fell silent, waiting expectantly.

"Would you care for another recitation?" asked Memory Nobbs.

"YES!" roared the miners.

Memory Nobbs frowned.

"Yes what?"

The miners dropped their eyes, and shuffled their feet.

"Yes, please," they mumbled.

"Then," cried Memory Nobbs, "by popular request, and following his recent astounding success, that versatile versifier, that pocket-sized poet, that rollicking rhymester, Klondike

Arthur, returns to our stage WITH ANOTHER NEW POEM!"

Amid the whistling and cheering, Arthur climbed onto the table. He turned to Memory Nobbs.

"Funny or serious?" he asked quickly.

"Funny, I think," replied Memory Nobbs. "You've put 'em in the mood. Another sad poem, and they wouldn't know where they were."

Arthur moistened his lips; the crowd got quiet.

"This one is another short poem," he said, "also about Alaska. It's called 'An Amazing Bit of Digging,' by Arthur William Foskett again:

"I have heard there was never a finer
Man at digging than one Klondike miner
    Who started from here,
    Dug straight down for a year,
And eventually came out in China!"

The audience was still crashing into the furniture and shrieking its head off when Klondike

Arthur, quietly and thankfully, slipped away to bed.

Within the week, Dogsnose Gap was the most famous town in Alaska, and Klondike Arthur was its most famous citizen.

Night after night, the Rotten Old Saloon was packed not only with local prospectors but also with men who had come from many miles away to listen to the boy whose fame had somehow spread to every gold field, mining camp, and shanty town in the territory. And not the sort of men, either, you would immediately think of as poetry lovers; but the fact of the matter is that none of them had ever listened to poetry before. They had always considered it sissy and never realized that it had anything to do with real life at all.

But it truly *is* about very real and ordinary things, as the miners found out: Arthur recited poems about being afraid and about being lonely and about being happy and about being lucky. He had poems about the cold and about the heat, about food and about animals, about home and about children — in short, Arthur had poems on just about every subject there was. And when he had finished one, whatever it was about, there was always somebody sitting in the Rotten Old Saloon who would nod his head and wish he'd said that, because Arthur had managed to put into words what so many of them felt or thought.

And, do you know, their behavior actually improved? Memory Nobbs was the first to notice that they weren't quite as rude or as angry anymore, and it certainly didn't take Memory Nobbs to notice that far fewer people were getting shot. All this may just have been because Klondike Arthur's poetry had a way of making people feel that there were more important things in life than money, and certainly that there were more important things to get shot over than a dirty look or wanting someone else's boots!

In fact, sometimes when trouble looked as though it was about to start, Arthur would quickly think up a poem on the spur of the moment. It was usually one of his funny ones, and everybody would laugh and put their guns away and shake hands, and the trouble would be over before it had even started.

For example, one night a number of miners from another town rode in on their mules. They stomped into the Rotten Old Saloon, and boasted, very stupidly, that they could drink more than any man in Dogsnose Gap. Now the Dogsnose Gappers were very proud of themselves, and as silly as they were proud, so that pretty soon everyone was drinking far more than was good for him. Hubert Tiddle soon rushed into the back room where Arthur and Memory Nobbs were eating steak pie and boiled potatoes, and yelled: "Do something

quick! They're all so drunk that any minute now the shooting'll start and there'll be blood all over my nice clean sawdust!"

So Arthur and Memory Nobbs put down their knives and forks and hurried into the saloon, and Memory Nobbs whispered: "Have you got a poem about how silly it is to get drunk, Klondike Arthur?"

And Arthur thought for a moment and said: "No, but give me a minute, and I will have!" He began to turn rhymes over in his head frantically while Memory Nobbs beat on the table with his shoe, so that everyone stopped arguing and looked at him. It was just in time, too, since a number of pistols were glinting wickedly in the lamplight, and a number of horrible-looking knives were flashing bright darts on the ceiling.

". . . proudly present Klondike Arthur!" called Memory Nobbs's voice into the sudden silence, and Arthur mounted his usual table.

"A short poem entitled 'The Trouble with Drinking Too Much,'" announced Klondike Arthur, "by Arthur William Foskett."

He cleared his throat.

"A drunken prospector called Bruce
Once climbed, by mistake, on a moose!

And yelled, 'This darned bike
Makes a noise I don't like,
And the handlebar's terribly loose!' "

Well, of course, the miners not only began laughing, the way they always did, they also realized, a bit sheepishly, that Arthur was riding them a bit. So they looked at one another and grinned, and it was all right, after that. The drinking slowed down somewhat, and Hubert Tiddle could breathe again.

But not, unfortunately, for long.

Because, on the very next night, just as the Rotten Old Saloon was settling down for the evening to a little fun and relaxation, with Klondike Arthur reciting to a packed and cheering audience, the door which had been flung open on an earlier fateful occasion was suddenly flung open again!

With the same terrible force!

By the same terrible man!

Arthur, who was halfway through one of his rather sad poems about a dog that was stuck down a rabbit hole, stopped in mid-line. Across the length of the huge saloon, the awful eyes of Grizzly Wilkinson burned straight at him!

"GO ON!" cried the audience. For they had been so absorbed in the poem that they had not heard the door crash open, nor felt the blast of Arctic cold.

"AND," roared Grizzly Wilkinson, as though he were just adding to the last words he had spoken a month ago, "IF THERE'S ONE THING I HATE EVEN MORE THAN MUSIC, IT'S POETRY!"

One or two of the more cowardly miners fainted!

At least three screamed!

The rest just turned their heads, very slowly, praying that they had made a mistake; and, when they realized they hadn't, got very, very pale indeed.

As for Hubert Tiddle, he dropped to his knees, put his fat little hands together, and closed his eyes.

But Klondike Arthur neither screamed, nor fainted, nor prayed, nor even got the faintest shade paler. He simply stared straight back into Grizzly Wilkinson's eyes, and said quietly: "Then I can't see why you've come. You're welcome to stay and listen, of course, but if you're going to keep interrupting like that, then I'd much rather you turned around and went out again."

All together, the miners rolled off their chairs and slid under the tables! Nobody had ever spoken to Grizzly Wilkinson like that and lived, and it would be only a matter of seconds

47

before Klondike Arthur was splattered all over the walls!

Indeed, Grizzly Wilkinson's huge yellow eyes were rolling like marbles in a saucer. His furious breath whistled through his beard like a bitter gale in a dark forest. His great hairy hands went to his guns, and his giant thumbs clicked back the hammers as the guns flashed up toward Klondike Arthur!

They stayed there for a very long second, until, suddenly, the thumbs eased the hammers down again, and the hands slid the guns back into their black holsters.

The miners, fingers in their ears, peered out from beneath the tables, not believing their eyes. And then Grizzly Wilkinson broke the dreadful silence: "I don't think I will shoot anybody today," he said. "Because the last thing I want is a mess all over my saloon!"

The crouching miners unstopped their ears. Surely Grizzly Wilkinson hadn't said what they thought he'd said?

Arthur, his heart still clattering despite the brave look on his face, was the first to reply.

"What do you mean, *your* saloon?" he said.

Grizzly Wilkinson reached inside his bearskin coat, took out a large leather pouch, and tossed it onto a table.

"While some people were singing," he said, very sneeringly, "and while some people were listening to *poetry*, other people were digging!"

"He's struck gold!" whispered the miners, from the floor. *"Grizzly Wilkinson has struck gold!"*

"RIGHT!" roared the giant. "And do you know what I'm doing with my first bag of it? I'm buying this saloon, that's what!"

"Oh, *are* you?" inquired Klondike Arthur stoutly. "Mr. Hubert Tiddle might just have something to say about that!"

Grizzly Wilkinson threw back his huge head and laughed. And terrible though his roar was, and even more terrible his growl, both were nothing compared with his terrible laugh!

"Oh, might he, though?" he said. He snatched up the pouch of gold again and hurled it across the room to the trembling Tiddle, who staggered with the weight as he caught it against his belly. "I'd like to buy your saloon, Tiddle," said Grizzly Wilkinson. He took out his guns again. "I'm offering a fair price, but, of course, if you refuse, then it obviously won't be *my* saloon, and" — here he paused, spinning his revolvers on his enormous forefingers — "I won't mind making a mess all over it!"

Hubert Tiddle, who had gone by this time from white to pale green, nodded vigorously.

"It's yours!" he shrieked.

"Thank you," muttered Grizzly Wilkinson. "I've always wanted a saloon of my own. Nice little business, regular money coming in, *and*" — his glaring eyes swiveled about the room — "a place I could come to in the evenings, a nice quiet place, without nasty music, without horrible poetry, without a lot of rowdies charging around and annoying people!"

Beneath their tables, the miners groaned to themselves, for they dared not groan out loud. So that was what was to become of their lovely Rotten Old Saloon: a place without entertainment and without fun, where everyone had to walk on tiptoe and speak in whispers in case the owner got annoyed and started shooting his customers! And there was no chance that anyone would dare open another saloon across the road, not when they had Grizzly Wilkinson to compete with.

Life in Dogsnose Gap, reflected the miners wretchedly, was going to be pretty grim from now on. Not that they had much time to think about it, since Grizzly Wilkinson suddenly struck one of the tables with his pistol butt and roared: "COME ON! IT'S TIME EVERYBODY STARTED DRINKING! YOU'RE NOT SPENDING ANY MONEY DOWN THERE!"

One by one, the unhappy miners crept out from their hiding places, stood up, and began to walk miserably toward the bar.

After that, life in Dogsnose Gap was even grimmer than they had anticipated. The gloom that descended on the Rotten Old Saloon spread through the town and the mining camps; no fresh faces traveled across the wastes to visit them. What was there to visit? Not only were they not allowed to sing, or listen to poetry, they weren't even allowed to shout or fight or tell jokes, or put mice in one another's pockets or beetles in one another's drinks, or tie one another's shoelaces together under the tables, or do any of the silly things they had always done for a laugh.

Even the joy at making a gold strike wasn't what it had once been, since they couldn't throw parties in the saloon to celebrate. As for the poor prospectors who toiled all day in the freezing weather for no reward at all, imagine how they felt in the evenings, sitting in the

gray grim gloom of the Rotten Old Saloon, staring at the sawdust with nothing to take their minds off their disappointments.

To make things worse, Grizzly Wilkinson had painted the whole place dark brown, inside and out; dark brown being his favorite color, though (of course) nobody else's.

Then a curious thing happened, or perhaps I should say didn't happen. It had become Grizzly Wilkinson's habit to drop into the Rotten Old Saloon every morning on his way to his mine, and every evening on his way back, just to make sure no one was laughing or singing. But one Tuesday, about three weeks after he had bought the saloon and poor Hubert Tiddle had fled back to San Francisco, Grizzly Wilkinson did not come in at all, neither in the morning nor in the evening.

And when he didn't appear on the Wednesday morning either, the miners began to wonder.

"It's just one of his nasty tricks," said Memory Nobbs to Klondike Arthur, as they washed the dishes in the kitchen of the Rotten Old Saloon. Dishwashing was the only work for which Grizzly would pay them, and pay them very little at that, now that they were no longer allowed to be entertainers.

"Yes," said Arthur, drying a plate very carefully. "He's probably hoping that people will think he's stopped coming in, so that they start laughing or telling jokes or something, and then he'll suddenly burst in and catch them at it."

Memory Nobbs shuddered at the idea.

"Just suppose," he murmured, "if we . . ."

He never finished. For at that moment there was a shout so loud, and from so many voices, that Memory Nobbs froze in terror, thinking that the strain had been too much on the customers at last. Now Grizzly Wilkinson would seize the opportunity he had so cunningly

54

planned and charge in to do unimaginably terrible things to the poor wretched miners next door! He and Arthur looked at each other, horrified, then tore off their aprons to run inside and see if they couldn't stop the row before it was too late!

The scene that struck their astonished eyes was even worse than they had imagined: the shouts had turned to cheers in the space of a second, and now the miners were rushing

about the saloon and jumping up and down on the tables and throwing bottles through the windows, and rolling about on the sawdust, laughing hysterically, and doing all sorts of things likely to have Grizzly Wilkinson shooting them by the dozen!

"STOP!" yelled Memory Nobbs. When they didn't, he whistled his famous whistle, and Arthur banged a brass saucepan with an iron ladle, which he had sensibly thought to snatch up as they ran in from the kitchen.

At last, the crowd fell silent, panting and grinning.

"Are you crazy?" cried Memory Nobbs. "He'll turn you into mincemeat! He'll feed you to the wolves!"

"THAT'S ALL *YOU* KNOW!" thundered Ironface Sam McGhee, the happy sweat running down the channels of his scars like raindrops on a wrinkled rock. "GRIZZLY WILKINSON IS DEAD!"

"*Dead?*" cried Klondike Arthur.

"As good as, anyway," replied Ironface Sam McGhee. "He's trapped in his mine, and he's been there for two days now. We just heard from Small Ned Chubley who rode past the Wilkinson mine this morning and saw the shaft all closed up with fallen rock. He must have dug too far in without making sure he'd propped the roof up securely, the greedy old pig, and it serves him right!"

"HURRAH!" cheered the miners.

"Wait a minute," said Klondike Arthur sharply. "Do you mean to say that he's still alive, or may be, at any rate, and here we all are doing absolutely nothing about it?"

"That's right," said Small Ned Chubley, who was only about an inch taller than Arthur, "and a good thing, too."

"But we can't just let him die!" cried Arthur.

"Why not?" exclaimed Ironface Sam Mc-Ghee, and all the others nodded. "Do you think he'd risk *his* life to save any of *us*?"

"That," said Arthur firmly, "is not the point. He's more terrible than we are. If we just let him die, then we're making ourselves as terrible as he is. Don't you see?"

The miners fell silent, dropped their eyes, grew sullen, shuffled their feet, sniffed.

"Well, all right," muttered Ironface Sam McGhee. "I guess we ought to ride out and take a look."

"WURRRGH!" grumbled the miners.

"He's probably dead by now, anyhow," said Memory Nobbs, just to cheer them up; though he secretly hoped that Grizzly Wilkinson wasn't, because he felt the same way as Klondike Arthur did.

So they all climbed into their heavy outdoor clothes, and pulled on their great sealskin boots, and tugged the fur flaps of their brown beaver hats down over their ears, and trooped out onto the crunching snow. They collected their mules, and set off out of town, toward the Wilkinson mine, with Klondike Arthur and Memory Nobbs (who didn't own mules) riding high on the buckboard of the open hearse of Thinny Skrimmerlinnet, the undertaker.

It must be said, unfortunately, that Thinny Skrimmerlinnet was actually humming to himself as he drove his two black horses. For he was thinking that Grizzly Wilkinson's would be a very expensive funeral indeed, considering the outsize coffin he would have to have, and the fact that he was (or, hoped the undertaker, that he *had been*) a very rich man indeed, and would leave plenty of money to pay for such trimmings as brass handles, a marble tomb-stone, and possibly a big tip for everyone who turned up to bury him.

Certainly, when the long winding procession finally stopped at the entrance to the Wilkin-son mine, Thinny Skrimmerlinnet was sure that the funeral would take place. For where the wide black gap of the entrance had once been, with the shaft leading from it into the side of the huge snow-covered hill, there was now only a pile of great gray-black rocks, broken into enormous slabs like giant dominoes, com-pletely blocking the way into the mine.

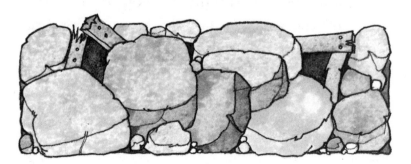

Everyone dismounted, and there were many sighs of relief, but none from Klondike Arthur, who lost no time at all.

"What we need," he cried, "is a block and tackle, and ropes, and pulleys! We'll have to haul the stuff up here from Dogsnose Gap, and build it as quickly as we can, that's if he hasn't frozen to death already. And then we'll need a . . ."

"Hold on there!" cried Ironface Sam McGhee. "First off, we'll have to chop down trees to make the tackle. Then we'll have to set up a forge right here to make the axles and the brackets, and we'll have to get a winch rigged up, and I don't know what else — some of those rocks weigh ten tons or more. All this is gonna take hours and hours. How do we know it's gonna be worthwhile? Even if he's still alive, by the time we get the gear working he could be dead from cold and hunger, even if he ain't got terrible injuries; I must say I don't see much point in . . ."

"Let's find out, then!" shouted Arthur, for he

had noticed something with his extremely sharp eyes: which was that although the rocks lay piled against and on top of one another, there were here and there small gaps between them, and as he clambered over them, it occurred to him that there just might be a way of contacting Grizzly Wilkinson. Cupping his hands to his mouth at each of a dozen different gaps, Klondike Arthur shouted the miner's name, and once or twice that name echoed back, suggesting even wider and deeper spaces beyond.

"Does he answer?" called Memory Nobbs, watching from below. "Can you hear anything?"

Arthur shook his head.

"HURRAH!" cried the crowd, in somewhat wicked relief, while Thinny Skrimmerlinnet rubbed his hands and began to make expensive calculations with a sharp stick in the snow. "Let's go home!"

"No!" shouted Arthur. "If we could get to him, take him a hot drink, or food, or blankets, tell him that help was coming, we might still be able to save him!"

"Get to him?" cried Ironface Sam McGhee. "Nobody could get through those cracks, unless he was a snake or something!"

Or a small, rather thin boy, thought Klondike Arthur. For while it was certainly true that no grown man, not even Small Ned Chubley (who made up in fatness what he lacked in height), could squeeze between the mighty slabs, there was a very slight chance that Arthur might manage it. While a chance did exist, however slight, Klondike Arthur was not the boy to give it up. So he slid and climbed and scrabbled down the rock pile again, grabbed a couple of pack blankets from the nearest mule, asked Ironface Sam McGhee for the bottle of whiskey he always carried, and turned back once more to the ruined mine.

"You're crazy!" cried a number of miners from different parts of the crowd.

"No, he's not," murmured Memory Nobbs, as he watched Arthur begin his climb, "he's just remarkably brave."

It was true. For who could tell that Klondike Arthur would not wriggle inside the first layer of rock, and even the second, only to get trapped inside the third, where no grown-up could reach him, or crushed by a sudden movement of the fearful rocks? And indeed, as he wormed and squirmed now, scraping his shins, tearing his hands, and bruising his whole body (for even the thick winter clothes were no protection against the razor-edges of broken rock), Arthur felt for the first time a cold fear strike through him. It was black, utterly black, now, in the heart of the rock maze. He could hear the grisly grinding as the rocks settled, and he suddenly realized that he had no room to turn around, so that he could not go back, could not get out, but only wriggle and twist and scrape

his way forward, pushing the blankets before
him, praying that each time a fresh layer of ap-
parently solid rock appeared he would somehow find a large enough gap to drag his aching
body through.

And, amazingly, he did!

Until, suddenly pushing between two huge
boulders like twenty-ton buns, he found himself falling, turning in the air, and, luckily,

landing with a thump upon the roll of blankets that had dropped beneath him.

He could see nothing. But he could hear something. Breathing!

Klondike Arthur crawled toward the sound, and suddenly recoiled as his hand touched some unseen hairy animal with huge teeth!

Shuddering, he lit a candle and found that what he had touched had been the huge bearded face of Grizzly Wilkinson!

Who stirred now, and groaned, but rolled over and would not open his eyes.

"I am going to die," he croaked, in the faintest of whispers.

"Nonsense!" cried Klondike Arthur sternly, and grasping Grizzly Wilkinson's hair in both hands, he pulled him up into a sitting position, uncorked the whiskey, and shoved the bottle into the man's mouth between his blue and frozen lips.

Grizzly Wilkinson spluttered, then he coughed, then he drank, then he guzzled! He opened his eyes. He stared at Arthur.

"*You!*" he gasped. "Why would *you* come to rescue *me?*"

"Don't talk!" snapped Arthur. "Save your strength. Help is on the way; they're building a block and tackle to lift the rocks off, but it'll take a few hours, and we've got to keep you warm."

And so saying, he wrapped Grizzly Wilkinson in the blankets, and made him drink more of the warming whiskey, and even — just imagine it! — snuggled up against him so that some of his warmth would help take the chill off Grizzly Wilkinson's shivering body. And

gradually, as he began to think that he might not die after all, Grizzly Wilkinson gazed at Arthur with those huge yellow eyes of his, which shone like a lion's in the flickering light of Arthur's candle, and he murmured quietly: "Nobody has ever done anything like this for me in my entire life before."

Which, thought Arthur, probably went a long way toward explaining things about Grizzly Wilkinson. But what he said was: "It's hardly surprising, considering the way you treat people!"

But instead of losing his temper, Grizzly Wilkinson just nodded.

"You're right," he said, "you're absolutely right."

And then Grizzly Wilkinson, the most terrible man in all Alaska, began to cry.

"Oh, come on!" cried Klondike Arthur. "If we get sorry for ourselves, we're done for. Tell you what, let's sing a song to cheer ourselves up."

But Grizzly Wilkinson merely sniffed, and shook his head.

"I can never remember words," he said, "that's why I don't like music. I always get one song mixed up with another."

"My goodness!" cried Klondike Arthur. "I know a poem about someone just like you." And before Grizzly Wilkinson could remind him that he didn't like poetry either, Arthur began:

"There once was a miner called Bing
Who, when anyone asked him to sing,
Replied, 'Ain't it odd?
I can never tell "God
Save the Weasel" from "Pop Goes the King"!'"

Well, for perhaps the first time in his life, Grizzly Wilkinson produced a laugh that was not only not terrible at all, it was really rather wonderful, a great booming chuckle that echoed through the cave and made Arthur laugh, too, even though he'd recited the poem a hundred times.

"Was *that* poetry?" gasped Grizzly Wilkinson, when he had finally finished laughing. "I never realized poetry could be such fun!"

"Well, then," said Klondike Arthur, "perhaps we ought to try singing, too."

So they did.

When the block and tackle shifted the last enormous rock some six hours later and the white afternoon light flooded into the shaft, the mob of rescuers could not believe their eyes, nor their ears!

Klondike Arthur and Grizzly Wilkinson were sitting side by side with their backs to the wall, singing "Polly Wolly Doodle"!

And before the rescuers had recovered from the shock, there was another. For Grizzly Wilkinson, his huge strength almost fully returned, leaped to his feet and began to shake their hands and clap their backs and hug them, throwing his arms around four of them at a time!

They all rode back to Dogsnose Gap, singing as they went — with the one exception, I'm afraid, of Thinny Skrimmerlinnet.

As soon as they reached the Rotten Old Saloon, Grizzly Wilkinson announced that everyone could drink as much as he liked absolutely free, to celebrate the fact that he was going to repaint the place in yellow and white, *and put in a carpet!*

So they drank and laughed and drank some more, and Klondike Arthur recited eleven different poems and allowed himself to stay up until nine o'clock. Everybody had such a wonderful time that none of them noticed that late in the evening, after Arthur had gone at last to bed, Grizzly Wilkinson had once more disappeared.

He was gone for three days, and this time the miners were really worried. For they had generally agreed that the new Grizzly Wilkinson was a very fine fellow indeed, so much so that search parties went out to look for him day and night, but with no success.

Until suddenly, at around lunchtime on the third day, just when the miners were plunging back into the despair from which they had so recently been rescued, the doors of the Rotten Old Saloon opened, and Grizzly himself burst in. And, as opposed to the last time he had done any door-bursting, this time his face was lit by an enormous smile as his mighty arms dragged something behind him into the room. The thing was covered in a sheet, but not for long; for, as the miners gazed, Grizzly Wilkinson snatched the sheet away, and there in the middle of the newly carpeted floor was the finest piano they had ever seen!

"Good heavens!" cried Memory Nobbs. "I'd know that piano anywhere! It belongs to No-Nose Muldoon!"

"Not anymore it doesn't," replied Grizzly Wilkinson.

Klondike Arthur gave him a specially stern look.

"You don't mean," he said, "that you — "

"I know what you're thinking," said Grizzly Wilkinson, "but you're wrong. I paid for it with good yellow gold."

"A piano again!" shouted Memory Nobbs, sitting down at it immediately and running his fingers lovingly along the keys.

"Thank heavens!" exclaimed Arthur. "I had just recited my one hundred and forty-seventh poem. I was wondering what to do next."

He was so relieved to have that particular weight off his mind that he began to whistle.

Which made Memory Nobbs fall clean off his stool!

"THAT TUNE YOU'RE WHISTLING!" he yelled. "THAT'S *IT!*"

"You mean," said Klondike Arthur, "the one you can never remember? Number one thousand two hundred and thirty-four?"

"YES!"

"Are you sure?"

"OF COURSE I'M SURE!" cried Memory Nobbs, jumping up and down impatiently. "For heaven's sake, *tell me what it's called!*"

Grizzly Wilkinson suddenly beamed his proudest grin.

"*Everybody* knows that!" he roared. "It's called 'Pop Goes the Weasel'!"

And he gave Klondike Arthur a very special wink.